THIS BOOK BELONGS TO:

LIMITED EDITION

TOMMY JAKES
An Imprint of Dexterity Publishing
www.TDJakes.com

Illustrations by Tim Collins
Cover Design and Layout by Eileen Rockwell

ISBN 13: HC 978-0-7684-5020-0

For Worldwide Distribution, Printed in the U.S.A.

1 2 3 4 5 6 7 8 9 10 11 / 23 22 21 20 19 18

CHAPTER ONE

The Special Day

Ring, ring, ring!

It was 7:00 a.m., and the sound of Sasha's alarm clock reminded her of the excitement this school day would bring.

"Yay!" Sasha shouted. It was Show and Tell Day in her second-grade class, and she could hardly wait to share the special birthday necklace that her grandmother had given her.

Sasha darted to the bathroom to wash her face and brush her teeth. She was already dressed when her mother checked in on her.

5

6

"Wow! Look at you! You're up all by yourself! I guess you are being more responsible now that you're 8 years old?"

"Oh Mom, don't be silly," Sasha laughed. "I am just really excited about today! I can't wait to show everyone the special cross necklace that Grandma gave me. The beads make it so pretty!"

"Okay sweetie," said Sasha's mom. "Just remember to take it off before recess and put it in your backpack like we discussed."

"Okay Mom!" Sasha shouted as she whooshed down the stairs for breakfast.

CHAPTER TWO

Show and Tell

"And that's why this necklace is so special." Sasha beamed as she showed the class the 8 beautiful beads on the necklace at the end of her Show and Tell presentation.

As Sasha returned to her seat, Mrs. Griffin asked the class to clear their desks before recess. Sasha remembered what her mother said and tucked the necklace safely into her backpack.

All the children went outside to play, except for Rachel and Blake, who had to finish their writing assignment before going out.

13

CHAPTER THREE

The Missing Beads

"We are finished with today's math problems," Mrs. Griffin told the class at the end of the school day. "It's time to go home now, so please pack your bags and prepare for dismissal."

As Mrs. Griffin erased the board, she was startled by a frantic cry.

"Oh nooooo!" cried Sasha. "What happened to the beads on my necklace?" Sasha's eyes began to well up with tears. "I put my necklace safely away in my bag before recess, but now all the beads are gone." Sasha looked very, very sad.

"Class, does anyone know what happened to Sasha's necklace?"
Mrs. Griffin asked.

All the students shook their head "no"-except for Rachel and Blake.
They were both looking down at their shoes.

"Rachel...Blake...is there something you want to share?" Mrs. Griffin asked. They continued to look away sheepishly. Mrs. Griffin dismissed the other students and asked Rachel and Blake to stay behind, along with Sasha.

CHAPTER FOUR

Forgiveness

Once the other students left, Rachel blurted out, "Oh Mrs. Griffin, I am so sorry! The necklace was so pretty that I wanted to see it again. So I pulled the necklace from Sasha's backpack while she was at recess."

Blake spoke up also. "Mrs. Griffin, I am really sorry too. When Rachel got the necklace from Sasha's bag, I began teasing her because I didn't see why the necklace was so special. When I grabbed it from Rachel, the necklace fell to the floor and the beads came off." Even though Blake and Rachel looked very sorry, Sasha was very angry!

"Well," Mrs. Griffin said, "you both know that it's not right to take something that belongs to someone else. I know you didn't mean to break the beads off, but they are gone, and now Sasha is very upset. Do you know where the beads are?"

Blake pointed to his desk. "They are inside my desk," he said quietly.

Mrs. Griffin got the beads from the desk and smiled. "Look Sasha, the beads didn't break! Your necklace can be fixed!" Sasha sighed with relief, but she was still very mad.

Blake and Rachel looked at Sasha. "We are very sorry for what we did to your necklace."

Sasha stared down at the necklace. Her brow was still furrowed, and she was silent for what seemed like an eternity!

Suddenly, Sasha looked up at Blake and Rachel with a big smile! They were both puzzled. "You're not mad anymore Sasha?" Rachel asked.

Sasha hesitated.

25

"Well, I guess I am still a little mad, but I just remembered something Grandma told me, and I now understand what she means. So, I am smiling because my necklace means even more to me now, all because of what you did!"

Rachel and Blake were really confused now.

"You see, I learned from Grandma that the cross is special because Jesus died on the cross so that my sins can be forgiven. Even though he didn't do anything wrong, he died for me and for all of us. The only thing he asks is that I forgive others who do wrong things to me just like I have been forgiven. So, I forgive you! Now I understand what this cross means! It's not the beads that make it special, it is what Jesus did that makes it special!"

Mrs. Griffin smiled very proudly at her three students. They learned a lesson on that day that was more important than anything she could have taught them!

For Discussion

- Have you ever broken something that belonged to someone else? How did it make you feel?

- Did you hide the broken item, or did you tell the other person?

- Has anyone ever taken something from you without asking? Were you angry?

- Why do you think Sasha was still mad for a while even after Rachel and Blake apologized?

- What do you think Sasha meant when she told Rachel and Blake "...my necklace means even more to me now, all because of what you did!"

Memory Scripture

"Forgive us our sins, for we also forgive everyone who sins against us" (Luke 11:4).

Life Lesson

Sometimes you will do wrong and need forgiveness, and sometimes other people will do wrong to you and you will need to forgive them.

Prayer

Dear Heavenly Father,

Thank You that Jesus died on the cross to forgive me of my sins. When others do wrong against me, help me to forgive them just like You have forgiven me. Help me to be like Jesus! Amen.

Glossary

- **BEAM** - to smile happily

- **FURROWED BROW** - an expression on someone's face in which their eyebrow is narrowed or wrinkled

- **SHEEPISHLY** - showing or feeling embarrassment because you have done something wrong

- **WHOOSH** - the sound made by someone who is moving quickly

CPSIA information can be obtained
at www.ICGtesting.com
Printed in the USA
LVHW07*1942200918
590848LV00003B/8/P